W0246871

This book belongs to

and

Teevra

TO OUR HUSBANDS

SACHIN NIK

AND

FOR ALWAYS HAVING A SENSE OF HUMOUR

© 2019 Little Ustaads Arts Private Limited
This edition published 2019

Published in collaboration with Bloomsbury India

ISBN 978-09-99403-31-0

Printed and bound at EIH Ltd., Gurugram, Haryana, India.

All rights reserved. No part of this book may be reproduced, transmitted or stored in an information retrieval system in any form or by any means, graphic, electronic or mechanical including photocopying, taping and recording, without prior written permission from the publishers.

www.littleustaads.com
www.bloomsbury.com

WRITTEN BY

Rachana Chandaria- Mamania and Kavita Bafana

NAMASTE DELHI

हौज़ खास DELHI METRO HAUZ KHAS

ILLUSTRATED BY

Sandhya Prabhat

Fasten your seat belt, we are about to land in India's capital city.
A sea of twinkling lights and buildings beneath us, New Delhi looks so pretty.

Delhi is a place to learn about government, culture and history.
Let's explore the town, visit the sites and uncover all its mystery.

We grab a large metro map and take the escalator underground.
It looks like a colourful spiderweb with lines all around.

We trace the lines to figure out our next station.
The metro zooms past. We begin our vacation.

We exit the metro and before us looms the Qutab Minar tower.

Built by rich Mughal Kings many centuries ago, when they held power.

We ride scooters past Humayun's Tomb, a grand monument
built for an Emperor who was patient and smart.
Emperor Humayun ruled for forty-eight years,
winning and losing battles but never did he lose heart.

Majestic Rajpath is filled with thousands of people parading towards India Gate Arch.
Today is Republic Day. We celebrate India's great freedom and join the glorious march.

Soldiers salute. Children wave flags. We sing Jana Gana Mana for the world to hear.
The yearly ceremony ends with jets spraying color in the sky so blue and clear.

We are running late to see the President. We race to his home.

The winner is the first one to reach and climb up the massive dome.

Rashtrapati Bhavan has over 300 rooms! Where could the President be?

We see him sitting in the green Moghul Gardens patiently waiting for us three.

We visit the Sansad Bhavan, where rules are made for each state
Leaders from all over meet here and work to make India great.

"Doesn't this building look like the wheel on the Indian flag?"
"Yes! The Bhavan is based on the Ashoka Chakra," I brag.

We grab kebabs and gol gappas from the Khan Market food stands.

Next, we nap at Lodhi Gardens and block the sun with our hands.

We head to Dilli Haat to buy gifts for friends back home.

There is lots to buy and Teevra gets a beaded comb.

Musicians play the sitar, tabla and veena at a classical show.

We watch the concert at the Indian Habitat Centre from the first row.

It's 4 am and fog covers the city
but we must wake up to catch our train.
We find our seats on the crowded Shatabdi Express
and wave from the window pane.

The Taj Mahal stands in front of me. It is by far the best building I have ever seen.
From the domes to the arches to the marble carvings, this place is surely fit for a queen.

"Excuse me, can you take a picture of my brother, my tiger and me?"
This will be the perfect memory to take home. We pose and smile with glee.

Agra Fort has big red walls and always protected the king.

Teevra loves the vast, open space and he starts to run and swing.

We continue our journey and see more Mughal homes, but this time it is behind a wall.
Fatehpur Sikri has many red buildings connected by stone steps, we better not fall.

In the cold night, back in Delhi, we see bonfires blaze.

People are enjoying the festival of Lohri and the end of winter days.

We don't have any Rupees left and head to the bank to get more.

Connaught Place is near, we can go pick up a lakh or a crore.

India is a free country thanks to Mahatma Gandhi, the father of our nation.

Standing tall and quietly at the Raj Ghat we bow our heads, and place a carnation.

Along the great Yamuna River, 1000s of people respectfully once stood.

Bapu's white dhoti and round glasses remind us of what is always true and good.

We hail a rickshaw and head to crowded Chandni Chowk, deep inside Old Delhi.

We smell hundreds of spices and taste the orange acchar, a mango jelly.

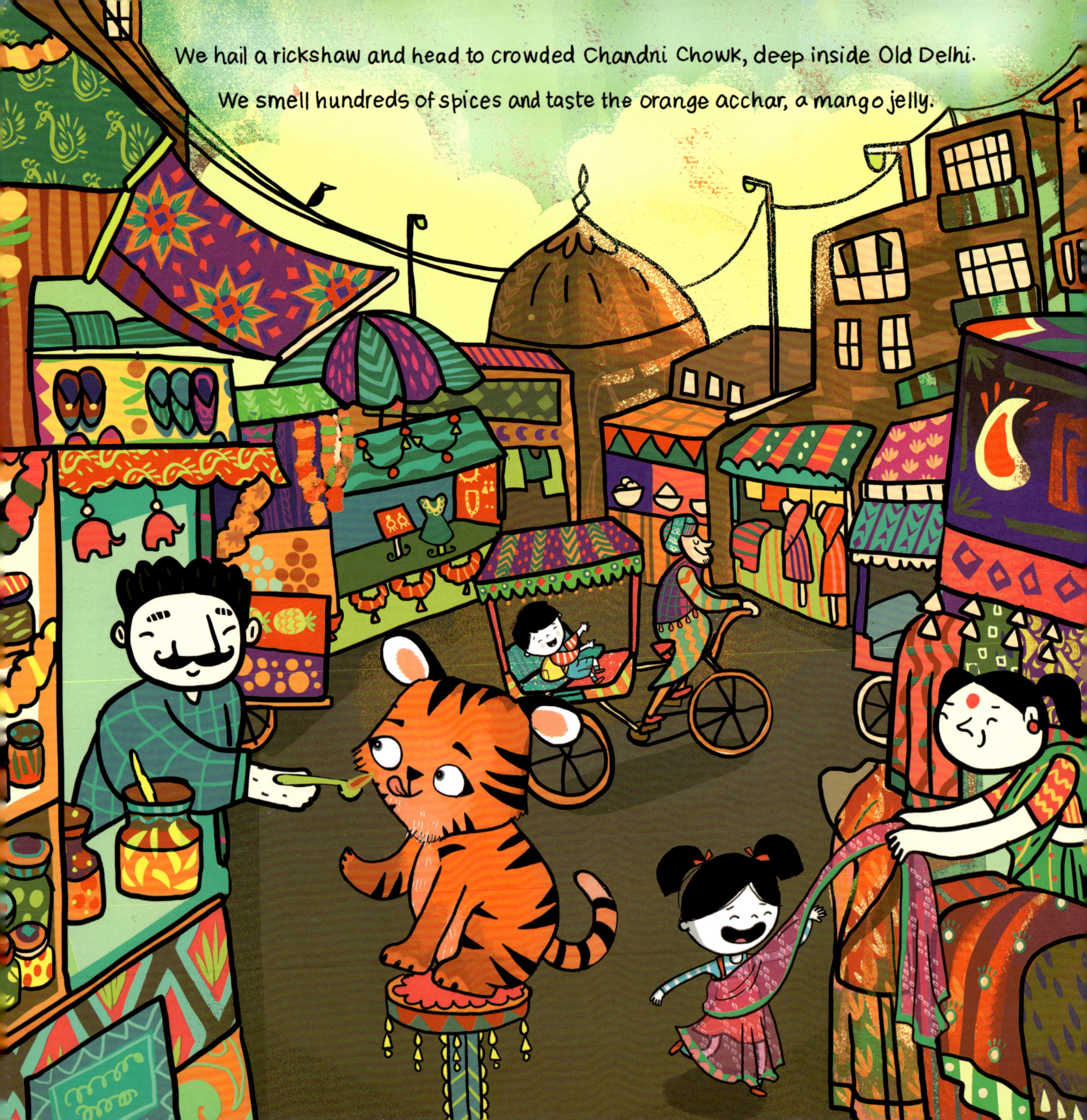

Crowds of people gather at Paratha Gali, to grab their hot lunch.

A cauldron bubbles with ghee as bread is fried, ready for us to munch.

Over 1 billion people travel to different parts of the country by trains.

At the National Rail Museum, some are diesel, some steam and some have gold chains.

Standing tall where all the roads meet,
is the magestic India Gate Arch.
The eternal flame burns brightly to
remember those who did once march.

The tour ends where Emperor Shah Jahan built the grand Red Fort.
Delhi became the capital and this Fort was the main court.

The mighty sandstone gates are tightly shut. Where can the main door be?
Teevra spots people next to the red wall paying the entrance fee.

The Red Fort is bright with color, painting the dark Delhi sky.
Voices tell us of India's rich history, some parts make us cry.

Delhi is a city that is bursting with stories of the past.

But it's time to go. We can't believe our trip has gone by so fast.

FACTS!

Delhi is the national capital of India.

Delhi was founded by Mughal Emperor, Shah Jahan, in the year 1649 and named it Shahjahanabad.

As early as in the year 1911, British announced to shift their capital from Calcutta to Delhi.

Delhi is famous for chaat and Mughlai cuisine.

Delhi's metro is India's first modern transportation system.

The world's tallest brick minaret the Qutub Minar is in Delhi.

Delhi has an International Toilet Museum which is run by Sulabh International dedicated to the history of sanitation and toilets.

Delhi was once a walled city which had 14 gates. Now only 5 among the 14 exist.

Khari Baoli market in New Delhi is the largest spice market in Asia.

In Delhi, the whole Public transport system runs on CNG.

It is the largest city in India in terms of area and the second most populated city in the world, after Tokyo

20 percent of Delhi is covered by forests

INDIA

NORTH

WEST   EAST

SOUTH

DELHI

ARABIAN Sea

BAY of BENGAL

INDIAN OCEAN

DELHI

Uttar Pradesh

RED FORT

Chandni Chowk

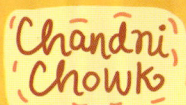
CONNAUGHT PLACE

India Gate

SAMSAD BHAVAN

RASHTRAPATHI BHAVAN

RAJPATH

YAMUNA RIVER

DOMESTIC AIRPORT

DILLI HAAT

LODI GARDENS

HUMAYUN'S TOMB

NOIDA

INDIRA GANDHI INTERNATIONAL AIRPORT

QUTAB MINAR

TUGHLAQABAD FORT

CHATTARPUR TEMPLE

GURGAON

HARYANA

PB 109827
20/11/24